12/10

This book belongs to:

_____

_____

_____

First published by Walker Books Ltd.,
87 Vauxhall Walk, London SE11 5HJ

Copyright © 2010 by Lucy Cousins
Lucy Cousins font copyright © 2010 by Lucy Cousins

"Maisy" audio visual series produced by King Rollo Films Ltd
for Universal Pictures International Visual Programming

Maisy™. Maisy is a registered trademark of Walker Books Ltd., London.
All rights reserved. No part of this book may be reproduced, transmitted, or stored
in an information retrieval system in any form or by any means, graphic, electronic,
or mechanical, including photocopying, taping, and recording,
without prior written permission from the publisher.

First U.S. edition 2010

Library of Congress Cataloging-in-Publication Data is available.
Library of Congress Catalog Card Number 2009929787

ISBN 978-0-7636-4752-0

10 11 12 13 14 15 16 CCP 10 9 8 7 6 5 4 3 2

Printed in Shenzhen, Guangdong, China

This book was typeset in Lucy Cousins.
The illustrations were done in gouache.

Candlewick Press
99 Dover Street
Somerville, Massachusetts 02144

visit us at www.candlewick.com

Maisy Goes on Vacation

Lucy Cousins

CANDLEWICK PRESS

Today Maisy is going on vacation. How exciting! Maisy is packing her blue suitcase to go to the seaside. She packs a sun hat, camera, and books. What else will she need?

Maisy walks to the train station.
The station is very busy today.
Look, there's Cyril! He is buying
the tickets.

All aboard!

The train pulls
away from the platform.

Maisy colors while Cyril chooses some snacks.

Everyone takes out their tickets when the conductor arrives.

Nearly there!

Can you see the ocean?

Maisy and Cyril go to their hotel room.
They bounce on the bed. Then it's
time to unpack
and go to . . .

the beach!

Splash! Maisy loves
to jump right in.

Splish! Cyril likes to paddle.

There's so much
to do at the
beach—

collecting
shells,

building
sand
castles,

playing all
day on the
shore.

Then it's time for
a snack. Maisy eats

ice cream, and
Cyril drinks juice.

Then they write postcards.
Cyril writes to Charlie. Maisy
writes to her friend Dotty.
"Our first day at the seaside
was lovely," she tells her.

At the end of the day, Maisy
and Cyril return to their hotel
room and get ready for bed.

Good night, Maisy.
Good night, Cyril.

Have a
nice vacation!